T0114695

Why
THEY
Cheat

M O U N A   M   F A L L

BALBOA.PRESS
A DIVISION OF HAY HOUSE

Balboa Press books may be ordered through booksellers or by contacting:

Balboa Press
A Division of Hay House
1663 Liberty Drive
Bloomington, IN 47403
www.balboapress.com
844-682-1282

Print information available on the last page.

ISBN: 979-8-7652-2705-3 (sc)
ISBN: 979-8-7652-2706-0 (e)

Balboa Press rev. date: 06/15/2022

This is why they cheat!

I decided to write this book in order to answer a few questions. Most people have so many concerns and misunderstandings about Loyalty.

Men and Women should be able to find some answers as well as some type of closure.

Now let's make it clear that I do not have all the answers. This subject is so vast. Neither, the most popular reasons have been definitely highlighted. I am aware of differences of opinions, denials, acceptances and accountability.

Therefore, all I do mostly is to spread the Love.

Contents

Preview

Let's define MAN!

After several research it came to:

Adult Male Human!

So to be a man, you have to first be an adult, then a male and I guess a human will do.

Now I have decided to define the word ADULT!

So after reviewing a few definitions I picked this one! Cause I like it!

Biologically, an adult is a human or other organism that has reached sexual maturity. In human context, the term adult additionally has meanings associated with social and legal concepts. In contrast to a "minor", a legal adult is a person who has attained the age of majority and is therefore regarded as independent, self-sufficient, and responsible.

Well at least we hope for the best.

Ok now what?

MALE

of or denoting the sex that produces small, typically motile gametes, especially spermatozoa, with which a female may be fertilized or inseminated to produce offspring.

I guess let's define HUMAN so we can move on!

Now that was not easy to find a definition I could truly appreciate so I went with this:

Of or characteristic of people as opposed to God or animals or machines, especially in being susceptible to weaknesses.

I will go over each detail of the definition as we move on with this book.

My definition of a man will be:

Weak Male Adult with a Sex to be only use as a gender locator.

To be fair I will use the same definition to describe a woman; simply replace Male by Female!

Just kidding Women don't cheat!

We can debate this all day long if you want to argue.

I have never ever ever seen a woman cheat, "periodtttt".

Yes!

Let me think about ...

Yes, final answer!

My definition of a man will be:

Weak Male Adult with a Sex to be only use as a gender locator.

Which I will refer to sometime in the book as a **W.A.S** instead of Man just for fun but mostly as a reminder, we still need them wonderful men.

After all, who will fix the plumbing issues?

The deal is that the majority of human wants to have sex, preferably with as many partners available.

Could be for the experience, the curiosity or simply for the pleasure. Therefore whenever the opportunity presents itself, it's a go.

Biologically it's imperative for any human to have sex with as many sexual partner as they physically can handle; originally in order to procreate as a survival natural instinct.

So sex in his act it's not necessarily a bad thing or an action under our control. We heard excuses as if I had enough at home I wouldn't cheat.

She seduced me.

I didn't know we were exclusive.

I can't do certain things with my partner.

There's something special about this girl.

I didn't know it would have ended up with sex and so on…

★ ★ ★

I am leaving space so you can add your own!

We have heard it all! Most of the excuses have been covered.

Now it's time to know the real reasons behind the treasons.

CHAPTER

One

#Number 1 Reason is due to the Lack of Social Support:

Social support is defined as an informant leading a person to believe that he or she is cared for, loved; esteemed also, who is a member of a network of mutual obligations.

A W.A.S may have been subjected to some sort of neglect behavior; from their parents or simply a lack of role model.

The Absence of leadership is one of the main reasons a W.A.S will not know where to start especially if they are a "follower type".

Their needs for supportive friendships with other men or women may have been undervalued.

In that case the entire expectation of his social and emotional needs fall entirely on their significant other.

Whenever inevitably they end up failing in that duty, the W.A.S will automatically seek fulfillment elsewhere.

Sadly a lot of men and women are not aware of those expectations.

They will never be able to take on that reversal role which will undeniably lead to Chaos and the end of a Peaceful relationship.

Let's create a visual by sharing an example about a real situation which I am sure many of you can identify with a similar story.

Angela was working as a customer service agent for a well renowned bus company.

Those buses you can take to go to New York for Ten Dollars round trip, yep one of those companies.

Keith was working for the same company and this is how they met.

Keith observed her every time he was servicing the bus. Meaning Keith was working for the maintenance department. This guy instead of focusing on changing the oil in these humongous buses and rotating those big tires, he was just observing Angela!

She was escorting a few passengers sometime and he could see her long legs stretching on the pavement.

She was always very classy, elegant and so sexy to his eyes.

Keith made a few mistakes at work getting lost watching Angela...almost lost his job on a few occasions.

This is what I was talking about, this Keith smh

Man! Focus! All I want to do, is to get to New York in one piece and get back home!

His friend Julio used to encourage him to talk to her but he was not ready.

Julio is the type of guy, straight to the point. Big flirt, always trying to get someone to try him out.

About 3 months after Keith first saw Angela, destiny was coming to a closure.

Keith was so slow, even destiny had to interfere. Like cupid has to step on the plate.

Out of nowhere, they met at the entrance at the start of their work shift.

Angela smiled and greeted him. He couldn't believe she said his Name.

"Wow she knows my name" he thought, smiling from ear to ear.

Keith thought he said that in his mind but he said that out loud.

Angela heard him. She must have killed his joy by reminding him that his name was tagged on his uniform. Keith stops smiling and stands there looking like an idiot while Angela proceeds inside.

Funny moment to me but a little devastating for Keith.

He is kind of sensitive when he is in love. I really wanted to say something else but I am a nice person.

Not sure what to do he just smiled. Shook his head from left to right. Seemed to shake it off and walked inside.

Keith decided to remember that specific time she walked in and will try again the next day.

Maybe I can start with a joke he thought.

The entire day he came inside the main building several times to use the bathroom or buy snacks from the vending machine.

Keith got so many snacks from his multiple trips.

Eventually Angela started to pay attention to him. I mean this Angela is something else too.

Honestly, I think these two "slow mo" belong together.

Keith was pretty handsome, 6"2,180lbs, 36 years old, beautiful bronze skin and his gray eyes were unique.

A chocolate man with Gray eyes, why was I working there myself smh

Julio couldn't take anymore after 5 months of this long and slow dance. He took matters into his hands since even cupid failed.

Julio decided to let Angela know that Keith would like to take her out to a movie; but really it would be a date.

Surprisingly for Julio, Angela was charmed and agreed.

Well she was eyeing Keith since the time she met him at the entrance.

He was wearing this fresh cologne which was still tattooed inside her nostrils.

Julio couldn't walk as fast as his short legs could let him.

With the excitement of a 3 years old finding his first Easter egg, he stood proudly in front of Julio.

"Guess what man" with a smile so weird, Keith thought this man was about to get punched.

"What Julio? I told you about those "guess what" games, I do not like them!

"Yah but you gonna like this one amigo"

Keith shook his head, deep down he really likes Julio like his brother. Julio always looks out for him at work, fixing his many mistakes due to his ADD brain.

"OK Julio, please what?"

"Your girl Angela said to call her for Y'all date"

Julio handed him a piece of paper with the most beautiful hand writing on it.

Keith was totally speechless! He was looking at those digits and instantly remembered them.

"Man wow, I don't know what to say".

Julio simply nodded with the proudest face ever and walked away with a swag Keith never noticed before.

Of course Keith took a break immediately, washes his hands and texted Angela so she can lock his number as well.

They started texting and calling all day.

They did go to the movie the next day and ended up at Angela's place.

I will spare you the details.

What? It's not that kind of book smh!

At work they were trying to play down low but not for too long. Keith ended up being fired anyway, one too many mistakes.

Well the Love story was getting stronger.

Keith was an excellent cook, and Angela loved food, a perfect combination!

Let's speed through the story, it seemed like those "slow mo" almost contaminated me.

My two love birds ended up moving together.

Keith decided to go to the community college in order to get more credits and a new certificate; while Angela will be picking up another job to keep up with the bills.

She refused for Keith to go to school and work at the same time because he was diagnosed with ADD.

She believed it was a recipe for failure and her man needed to succeed.

Everything works out well, Keith completed his master in Science, landed a great job in the veterans hospital meanwhile Angela got pregnant with their first daughter.

What an amazing love story, let me pull my tissues, eyes are getting watering.

Never any of my plans ever worked that well.

I am just saying, they may have ended up succeeding but not that easy.

They decided to get married but opted for a small ceremony with their closest friends and immediate family.

Julio couldn't be happier, he felt like a God Father.

Keith and Angela also honored him even.more when they told him they will name the baby after him, her name will be Julia.

If Julio owned wings, he would have flown away.

Luckily he couldn't but his new swag was showing his ultimate joy.

Close to the end of the pregnancy Angela had to stay in bed and Keith needed to take over the house and bills.

If you was bored now the actions are about to start

Well the cable ended up being cut off, notice of termination of utilities was piling up on the main table.

Angela and her now husband were arguing constantly.

She was frustrated that after 4 years of relationship she discovered a new Keith! Irresponsible, careless, liar, ungrateful and lazy.

Keith left the house more often because he was tired of the arguing and the drama Angela was putting him through.

In his mind her new name was Ms Drama Queen, no more my Queen, my Love or Love of my Life.

Keith couldn't believe what he signed for!

An angry woman, never satisfied, so demanding, acting like a diva of the future, so controlling!

She thought she was the man in the house, things had to be done her way or no way.

After all I am the man in this house, I don't need a woman to tell me what to do, how to do and when and where to do anything.

Keitj was less inclined to deal with the arguments and his new stressful home so he got a second job.

Julio used to tell him to be patient with Angela.

"She is pregnant and some pregnant women have their emotions on their sleeves".

Keith's answer was that Angela was crazy and Julio just doesn't know what he is going through at home.

Keith used to come home just to shower, change his clothes and leave right back to work.

One night, Angela, who was now at term, started to have contractions.

She was rushed to the hospital by Julio.

Sadly Keith was nowhere to be found.

They tried his cellphone a million times. Left billions of voice-mails.

Julio called both of his jobs.

The first one did he was off that day.

The second job stated that Keith left about a month ago and was no longer an employee there. Julio said to Angela that Keith was not reachable at the moment, he stepped in like the best Godfather Julia could have and held Angela's hands during the delivery.

Julio cut the umbilical cords and he was so emotional.

He doesn't even have any kid of his own.

He promised Julia to be there for her forever

Angela got a beautiful and healthy baby, she looks just like her daddy.

Angela was emotionally and physically drained.

This pregnancy was so hard.

Her family is still in North Carolina and no one will come for a day or two.

She just wanted to sleep. She couldn't even cry anymore.

Keith eventually showed up the next day without too much explanation.

Julio was disappointed in his friend. He tried to talk to him but Keith was so aggressive about the subject.

Keith was still only to come home, take his shower, change his clothes, hold his daughter for about an hour and leave for "work".

The routine went on for another month till Angela decided to find out what was the issue and discussed their relationship.

She asked Keith to take off work the next fay so they can talk Angela was so scared, she knew Keith was slowly leaving her.

She didn't recognize her King, the man of her dreams.

Keith was fading away and she was powerless.

She was depressed and her sister used to tell her it's normal after giving birth.

The following night, Keith did take off from work.

He showered, rocked his baby to sleep and sat down with Angela.

He chose the furthest away chair in the dining room, he kept avoiding eye contact.

She knew the signs of his behavior could mean that he was no longer involved in their relationship.

She was praying inside of her heart for God to intervene and change the outcome.

She was already silently crying before Keitg even said anything to her.

He was not even looking or acknowledging her wet face. He was flipping his phone unto his hands and looking at the front door like someone would come anytime soon to take him away.

They sat there in silence for a good ten minutes.

Keith broke the silence impatiently like he had somewhere to be and could no longer waste his time in this house.

Keith felt like a stranger at home. He felt "gauche" like the French will say.

Keith knew his time was up and this was his opportunity to go.

Keith decided to tell her that it was her responsibility to handle the house but she wanted to lay there and have babies.

Keith told her that she used to take care of herself, she used to look sexy and beautiful. She used to cook, clean, and help him with the bills but since she got pregnant, she has become lazy.

She stops everything and wants to boss him around, he is the Man in this relationship.

She stops having sex with him, they didn't even make love since she was five months pregnant.

He didn't marry a lazy woman, if he knew she would have made a 360 turn on him, he would have never married her.

Angela couldn't believe her ears.

She was sobbing like she never before.

Her heart was about to stop, she knew she was dying. Everything around her seemed black. She kept trying to open her eyes but she couldn't. She kept trying to open her mouth and say something but she couldn't. She was paralyzed, she lost entirely control of her functions. She could hear Keith going on and on with his complaints.

She didn't know how long she stayed in that dark cloud until she heard the last thing Keith said.

"I am done Angela, done with you and your bullcrap, I deserve a woman who can love me and respect me, I deserve a submissive woman not a woman who thinks she is a man!

You failed me Angela, you failed me"

Angela couldn't hold her anger and kicked his terrible loser self out.

She cried, cried and cried for days.

Her mother came and stayed with her for about a week.

Her mother called Keith and asked him to meet with her.

Keith came to see Angela's mom the next day of the requested appointment.

Angela was hopeful that since he came maybe he came to better senses.

They haven't talked since she kicked him out.

She did his laundry, cleaned the house, did her hair, nails and purchased a new outfit.

When Keith comes he will see how beautiful she is, she wants her husband back.

Julio has been a great support but he is like a brother to her, she needs her man.

They have a daughter together, they are married.

Keith was upset and neglected. She understood that and is willing to do better as a wife.

She should have never listen to the doctor.

She should have waited and save more money before getting pregnant.

It's hard for Keith, he has ADD and so many responsibilities she dumped on him was not fair to him. She deserves all Keith's said to her.

She can be submissive, he is her husband, she wants to be submissive to him.

In a few minutes, Keith will be here. She was so grateful her mom thought of calling Keith to invite him to talk.

She was even more surprised since her mom didn't say much to her but she knew her mom will get her husband back to her.

Keith came back for the meeting.

He was looking so good and smelling so good.

He reminded her on the first fay she met him.

She was smiling when she opened the door, she was met by a cold face.

She never knew Keith to be that cold.

Her husband must have been under a spell.

Her mother asked Keith to sit so they could talk.

He did that but sat on the dining chair like a stranger.

Angela informed him that she cooked dinner, his favorite meal and they can eat and talk after.

Keith declined politely and let them know that he had company waiting for him in his car outside and was hoping that could have been a quick meeting.

Angela was disturbed. He barely looked at the baby crib or asked about his daughter.

She assumed he was Julio and tell him he could let him in.

Keith got very upset, he told Angela's mom that this is exactly what he was talking about!

Right there, that bossy behavior, always telling him what he can or cannot do.

He was done with this marriage, her and her controlling self. He wants a submissive woman and she is not.

He only wants to take Care of his daughter, visit her.

He was done with Angela and he luckily met an amazing submissive woman who knows how to treat him with respect.

There we go Keith, you said it!

You find a submissive woman!

Keith cheated on his marriage.

Keith cheated on his wife.

Keith cheated on his daughter.

Keith cheated on the friends and family he swore in front of to love his wife for better or worse.

Once upon a time it was Angela, his Queen!

Today it is Lashante, his submissive woman.

Keith loved Lashante.

She understood him.

She succeeds where Angela failed.

She was also available whenever he needed her.

What will happen is Keith and Lashante's relationship will evolve and Keith will have more responsibility and eventually leave Lashante for number X, Y and Z.

This was Keith's second marriage, Angela thought Keith's first wife was lazy and was bossy.

Angela thought Keith's first wife didn't love him and took care of him.

She thought Keith's first wife had no compassion and disregarded Keith's handicap and put so much on him.

So she did better, she supported him, she acknowledged his handicap, she boosted him up so he can get a better life.

Today, Angela is Keith's second wife and she also failed him.

Today Lashante believed she is so much better than wife one and wife two and she is submissive.

She called Keith "Daddy".

She knows how to take care of her King, not like the others.

She doesn't talk to Daddy in any kind of way, she responds to Daddy's requests right away.

She is a better woman, she is Keith's woman now.

What will happen now is that Angela will get jealous.

Angela will be the "EX", the baby momma

He will stop coming to check on his baby because Angela is now becoming a witch.

I will say another single mother.

Angela didn't know that Keith was raised by a single mother. His mom handled all the responsibilities in the house, he went to the military at 18, got married at 22 for the first time. A few months after he was released from the army, he left his wife because he was overwhelmed.

Angela thought it was because Lashante was younger, or more successful, Lashante was just an exit.

As she was to the first woman Keith married.

Keith didn't know what it was to be a husband nor a dad.

He learned that the females are the ones who care and support.

His social support was from a female therefore his expectations are solely based on his upbringing.

Angela didn't know that Keith was A WAS.

She thought he was a mature male adult.

Keith didn't cheat because Lashante was better or Angela was a bad woman, Keith cheated because he was forced outside of his comfort zone into a reality he was not groomed toward.

Epic failure we may say but sad reality it is.

Some may ask what Angela could have done to prevent Keith from cheating?

Maybe Angela should have seen the Red Flags right before her eyes.

A man that was introduced to her by his best friend, like he needs someone to hold his hands.

A male she has to build into a Man but too quickly.

Sometimes we refuse to acknowledge the Red Flags but they are Red for a reason.

So when you are an Angela and you meet Keith, take it easy, less expectations or simply move to the right Man out there for you.

Love yourself, be accountable!

CHAPTER

Two

Reason #2 Misunderstanding of commitment

Following a little research it was not so hard to find two great definitions of commitment that I could use for this section.

Definition number one said:

The state or quality of being dedicated to a cause, activity, etc. Definition number two said: An engagement or obligation that restricts freedom of action. Now my W.A.S in this scenario is obligated to dedicate himself by restraining his freedom of action to please their partner....

Huuuummm let's see how that works!

W.A.S is expected to see the difference between romantic intensity relationships and long-term love based relationships.

W.A.S ultimately is becoming a victim of limerence which you can research and understand more by reading the book of Dorothy Tennov, a renowned psychologist.

***F.Y.I, I do not know the author nor that she paid me, I simply agree with her theorie so at each their own.

Eventually the neurochemical rush of romance in early love stories is replaced over time with less intensity, but ultimately more other meaningful forms of connection.

Sadly a W.A.S is not equipped to process those changes.

Michael learned the hard way after 3 years in jail for domestic violence.

Pamela was determined to be the best wife any man can have.

She has been targeting Michael since the last year of high school.

She had options but she wanted Michael.

The man was so ordinary, 5"9, a little overweight but he had the potential to be a Doctor and Pamela was very ambitious.

Michael was a nerd at school, his priority was his homework and staying above and beyond his grades.

Michael was raised by his uncle since he lost his parents at a very early age from drug addiction. He was very introvert and calm.

Never involved with any campus activities, and most importantly he has no known addiction.

Pamela on the other hand was a very beautiful and extra confident young lady.

Her Father was a judge.

Mom was this amazing and elegant stay home lady, a Homemaker.

Pamela was mixed with natural long silky hair.

Plus she was blessed by those rare and unique clear brown colored eyes.

She decided to be a NICU's nurse. We always need more nurses.

She loves babies but didn't want any so that was for her a great alternative.

Pamela and Michael went to the same college. Not sure how she got in but Daddy got ways where there's no way.

6 years later Pamela was done with college but Michael stayed for another 3 years.

Pamela was seen every day on campus, bringing dinner or picking up laundry.

The entire college knew Michael was taken, also no one really wanted him for his look.

Michael received a lot of support from Pamela's entire family.

Talking about a power couple.

Michael's uncle advised him to propose to Pamela since they have been dating for almost 10 years at this point.

Micheal has been dictated every step of his life with Pamela. Nothing was his own decision to make but a suggestion to comply with.

Typical Micheal did proposed on a set up organized by his uncle and Pamela's mom.

Of course to no surprise of us, Pamela said YES!

She didn't want to waste any more time.

The wedding was planned instantly and they got married asap.

More reasons too they were able to make it happen financially like yesterday.

The wedding was set in the Dominican Republic right at sunset.

Beautiful ceremony, 250 guests were able to make it. All the rooms in that magical resort were booked for the parties. The decoration was breathtaking..the thing is Pamela worked on it for years so eventually it was astonishing.

Nothing like the Dominican sky to give you the perfect background.

I mean where this sky is made from? Heaven?

The breeze was perfect enough to cool the guests but not messing up with make up and hair or shovel sand in your mouth.

Even the weather was compliant.

Michael was very stressed out. He didn't used ro mondaine ceremonies nor be the center of attention of so many people.

Pamela decided to order a massage for him in the room while she was enjoying the beach with the family and friends.

She was hoping Michael could relax so his smile can appear natural in the pictures.

The last session of pictures, Michale looks like he was kidnapped and was signing for help.

She remembered laughing so hard she almost fainted when she saw the pics.

Sandra was the masseuse, petite Dominican shaped like a guitar. Pamela never saw that masseuse. She ordered through room services, after all why worried, Michael knew she was a prize for him. Also he only has eyes for her. Michael never got a massage from none else than Pamela before. She used to massage his neck during the finals each year. He always thought of Pamela like a coach before you entered a ring or tight after you exit.

When he saw Sandra, he was thinking that his massage would have been very annoying checking her frele silhouette.

Little that you know, Michael ended up with a happy ending.

Sorry I had to skip, once again not that type of book! Lol

Boy I tell y'all!

Somehow he managed to have a massage everyday for the two weeks they were in the DR. He would check with Pamela schedule for the day and reach out to room service himself and request Sandra.

Why change what works.

Pamela was so busy entertaining her guests whom of course a good quarter of them stayed.

She didn't worry about Michael as long as he was seen with her for breakfast, lunch and dinner.

She was married to a Doctor, all she ever wanted.

Pamela could swear that Michael changes since they got married, some about his swag but she couldn't put her finger on the reason.

All she thought was he is proud of him and his priceless wife.

She could tell his bedroom performance was even upgraded.

Michael was not that boring anymore, he was experimenting.

If she knew marriage would have such an impact on this dude she would have married a long time ago.

Finally back to the U.S. they continued their routine. Pamela was no longer surprised by Michael's updates. She was happy that her married life would not be more boring than she predicted. Michael was working long hours as Pamela so they weren't really spending a lot of time together which was perfect for Michael.

He was very responsible, respectful toward his wife and responding to any of her demands or requests.

Michael was the perfect husband Pamela could have wished for.

Everything was simply amazing in the best of both worlds we could say.

Well it may be a perfect picture but if their story ended up in this book maybe it wasn't all of that!

So let's get into the messy part now

Somehow Pamela was planning to surprise her husband with the purchase of a boat, he loves boats. Like a little boy, he used to just go to the waterfront and stare at those beautiful yachts for hours.

He works so hard and since he was the perfect husband for Pamela why not surprise him for their anniversary.

She was showing off big time in front of her colleagues, friends, strangers, even her poor cousins that were still not married.

She works extra hours all this year to be able to afford a cash boat.

No financed deal for her hubby, she wanted the title to be his. No liens.

While checking on the online account to set up the purchase she accidentally found Michael personal bank account credentials log on. As a wonderfully curious wife she thought she could see what Michael is getting her for their anniversary. She started scrolling through the transactions thinking it won't be long before she can see what she is looking for.

Michael was so predictable. He never makes a purchase without telling her so the one she is looking for will be the one she never heard of.

She was right, she saw a strange transaction from a company she never heard of before. The awkwardness of these was the fact that they were repetitive.

What was he buying with so many small payments?

Why couldn't he just pay for it instead of making weekly payments? Michael may have been a need at school but in real life that man is not the smartest, she thought.

She started to wonder what those charges could have been. May be he was been scammed and she would end up with no gift or last minute stupid gift. She needed to get to the bottom of these mysterious money transfers.

She called the company to inquire about the charges.

A lady with some kind of Russian accent answered the call. She was told it was a spa service but no more information could be given to her concerning the type of clientele.

Pamela was in total distress, she called her mom immediately.

Mrs Carter was surprised but not alert as her son in law would go to a spa or Maybe was paying for someone. He was either at work or in the house, the man was involved in nothing, had no friends and was not a social person.

She advised her daughter to let it go and don't worry about it, she is sure Michael will get her a very expensive gift. She even promised Angela to check with Michael herself to ensure he got the right gift for their anniversary.

Pamela decided to confront her husband the same night regardless of her mom's advice to let go and keep moving.

She waited for Michael to get in bed and showed him the prints of his bank statements.

Michael was calm as usual, he told her that he was getting a massage from time to time when he needed it. She couldn't believe he hid this activity from her and felt betrayed. They could have shared that activity. She started to feel insecure suddenly when she realized Michael was able to do stuff without her. If he was able to conceal this, what else was he hiding from her?

They ended up falling asleep, so she decided to look into his iPad hoping to have more details on when he was going and what else he could have been doing.

What she found on the iPad was the end of her marriage.

She woke Michael up, and started to hit him.

Michael punched her by reflex, he didn't expect Pamela to be the one punching him so hard.

She ended up with a broken jaw as well as a black eye.

I am sure you are all wondering what made her snapped?

Michael has videos of females on top of him, nurses from the hospital, her best friend, her mother …...

Anyhow, Michael ended up in jail for domestic violence and all went downhill from that night.

With daddy being a judge, Michael's first offense was very severe. He was condemned to ten years in jail. Thanks to his uncle and the hospital staff who petitioned for his sentence to be reduced he ended up spending three years instead.

The main concern here is that Michael never understood the level of commitment he was expected to display.

Pamela's confidence prevented her from creating that passionate rush and maintaining it, she thought she was a prize for Michael, but Michael is just a W.A.S.

★ ★ ★

How could Pamela have prevented Michael from cheating?

Michael, if you ask me, was not at fault.

Pamela has been manipulative since she met him.

Pamela thought she was smart, a planner, she believed she had control over her life; which could have been true but her life and not Michael's.

Michael is an individual with his own want, aspirations and willingness.

The relationship was wrong from the beginning. Lack of passion, lack of boundaries, just a set for a dramatic play.

To me, Michael was a victim of a very manipulative woman.

Michael was also never mature enough to understand the intrinsic of a marital relationship. Who is it to blame? No one

Maybe the way he was instructed to propose, married, he should have been instructed in loyalty.

I mean Michael! Mama too???

When we meet someone, we need to be as natural, true and honest as possible. Real is rewarded, lies is paid forward, Karma is a B★★★h!

CHAPTER

Three

Reason #3 Immaturity:

Monogamy is not a shirt you can put on when it's cold and take it off when it's hot.

Immaturity: a W.A.S does not have a lot of experience in committed relationships.

A W.A.S does not fully understand that their actions will inevitably have consequences.

Some of those consequences can be as simple as emotionally hurting the partner.

The W.A.S may think it is fine to have one or more sexual adventures while in an existing committed and exclusive relationship.

The W.A.S might think of their commitment to monogamy as a jacket that they can put on or take off as it pleases, depending on the circumstances but we will say "excuses" instead of circumstances.

Just like a 2 years old, it will never be their fault! I am just a baby! Of course you are honey! Anyway, let's move on!

"John and I met on a dating site. I was just bored.

I feel like that sometimes, then I end up with nothing major to do.

So my solution is just going to sign up for a profile on a dating site!

I was probably on the site for about 15 minutes when I started to receive millions of requests...well look at me". Said Michelle laughing out loud and waving her hands from up to down.

Michelle was this petite blonde with big eyes full of eyelashes. Her tiny nose was making it hard to believe she got enough oxygen in her brain. Her beautiful curled lips seemed to never have a chance to rest. That girl could talk non stop for hours, I wonder if she has some kind of concentration disorder. Well it's not my call to diagnose this doll, I just have to read her cards, get my money and definitely I need a long break after her session.

"Are you listening to me?" she interrupted my short evasion from reality just on time.

"Yes I am listening to you so please continue Dear" .

"So I browsed the pictures of 100 gentlemen for about 30 minutes and went to bed. I was hoping to meet a few gentlemen, go to dinner then move on unless I find my prince charming right, you know what I mean right"?

I nodded with a large smile and a wink, that's all my girl needed to see in order to keep going with her monologue.

"He was technically better than all those other losers so I figured, I could hangout for a few.

I ended up talking to this stupid skinny dude, become friend with the one from Delaware but I realized I'm never gonna travel there.

Anyway there were some sparks about this other guy from New York. I thought he was rude at first but I realized it was a New York' swag.

The guy was named John.

John was so tall in the picture.

Also my impression when looking at his profile'pictures looks like he had a good time.

He seemed like he traveled around the world and I could see beautiful pictures from vacation probably taken in Taiwan; as well as other Islands based on the ship in the background. Also the Spanish looking food, like paella or the whole fried fish!

I was at home and he was traveling without me so I reached out to him. He responded the next day"

She finally took a long breathe for about 3 seconds.

"Guess what Sairah? I said Hey you look good and I would like to meet you, tease you and drop you. What do you think he said?"

Michelle was looking at me straight in the eyes at that moment I realized her eyes were Blue with some gold stars in them. She wasn't bad at all. Why was she single? She always smells so good, her hair has this unique baby scent.

She was waiting on me to actually say something!

"Please tell me "!

Without hesitating a second Michelle was back!

"He said to me... lady I am flattered but I need you to know that I have somebody, I'm not available" .

"I was so irritated! What are you doing on a dating website if you are not single? I asked him! right? so anyway I said before he could respond I just wanna be a friend with or without benefit!"

Now I knew he would fall for that, Sairah... she was holding her head and looking on the ground defeated.

He said no I don't need anymore friends right now michelle I am booked!

She stood on her little perfect legs, put her hands on her hips, stared at me like she was the one about to read me.

"Sairah, I was not about to let this handsome Portoricain reject me like that so I said yes! me too! I have a lot of friends but I want to jump your bones. I don't want another friend. I just really wanted one night with you".

My eyes were wide open, this Michelle is not going to stop surprising me. I had to sip on my now cold tea and started to burn some rosemary incense. Michelle was now talking for a full 30 minutes.

"Now he said OMGOSH! Girl"!

"I was so proud of me so I said what about we meet and we just have sex one time I'm just horny. He realized I was dead serious so he said I would love to just have sex with you! Because you are astonishing.

Sadly, I am not that kind of guy. Let's grab lunch, get some sandwiches, you know what we are going to have a date I'm going to decide after that if i want to have sex".

"We set a date where he took me to this nice restaurant and it was like an Italian setting. It was very romantic. We drank some wine and talked a lot and then I ended up in his bed.

Now while I needed more details Michelle was making it short smh

Oh wow this night was amazing. It was the best night ever! She continues...

We made love all night and I loved each and every second.

He said to me "I don't want a relationship, just go on a date, have sex, no string attach"...

"So I was looking at him like "what is he talking about right"?

Michelle tried to mimic his face and that was so funny.

"Well, I am dating a few girls. He proceeded to say and they all understand that I do not want any commitment. We all are getting along and we are having fun".

Sairah girl, she said with a pinch voice, "I guess" to sound ghetto!?!

"All I could hear was blah blah blah blah"!

Sairah I was like this man talk too much this is it!

I am done with that nonsense!

But you know it was so good, I like it so much I did it again two more times and then I stopped entertaining his shenanigans.

I told him "John since you're so busy I don't want to be a part of your little polygamist game, I deserve my own man so I will take my leave".

"He answered I don't want to lose you but I told you from the beginning I just don't want a relationship."

"I understand and I respect that is just going to be just that"

But in my mind, I knew that means I would just have to be anybody...

I told him, look Man, I want someone that wants to be with me so if you don't want to be with me it's fine.

What we are doing now it's just benefiting you!

I knew what it was from the beginning."

So he stayed quiet for a minute after he heard me and said:

"Yes but now I like you, I really like you, I wanna be with you and all this".

Girl lol, I put it on him like that!

And she made that weird laugh she does that freaked me out like another little mischievous four year old is about to appear.

"I was like dude we already said a lot I don't want just a fucking beautiful type of relationship"

"Of course eventually we end it, like broke up.

To my surprise Sairah, Jhon was not about to gave up on us.

The dude went ahead and also broke up with all the women and told me that from now on I was the only one".

Then he said, "you now know that I really like you.

Everything I needed in a woman you got it so I only want to be with you".

"Sairah, let me tell you it was a magical girl, it was unbelievable! I finally found my Man. I met his mother and he has 3 kids that I haven't met but you know I was thinking that would eventually happen!

My plan was to meet everyone and make them so happy. Of course I'm very upset and the reason I'm here now it's because this arrangement is not working. I love him more, he loves me more,well I think. We are talking and sharing a lot. I know him way too much. We are getting along as much as we are arguing. I want you to tell me what I'm supposed to do with him? Is he gonna marry me? how are we gonna be OK? what's going to happen in our relationship? can you please tell me? My friend kisha told me that you were so good at reading the future and that you will be able to tell me about Michael!

I guess it was finally my turn, my moment to shine and impress Michelle.

"Wow Michelle, what an amazing Love story"!

Michelle, you paid me to be honest, right?

She replied by noding her head.

"John is a narcissist"

Michelle's eyes widening but her mouth was shut.

He is not mature, he will play a co trilingual game with you, entirely. He could marry you but can you handle what you are asking?

Michelle was very quiet, she put hundred dollars on my desk, look at me for a good twenty seconds and walked out.

The strangest client I ever had. I mean she was babling non stop for one hour and now she shut her mouth.

My job is not to lie, I said what I know to be true.

… Long story short…

Michelle and John got together, they attempted several time to move in either homes but that didn't work.

John was manipulating Michelle like a marionette.

He claimed that he loves her and cannot live without her.

As soon as she fell for it, he stop answering his phone for an entire weekend. Of course Michelle will try to call him the entire weekend, worrying.

John is also a diabetic so she saw him going to a crisis of low insulin in his blood and it was not a pretty scene.

On Monday, John will appear back as if nothing never happen and candidly answer his phone.

After listening to Michelle's complaints, he would just say nothing! No explanation or apologies. Just nothing!

Michelle was going crazy with John's behavior.

She never was manipulated before. She was trying to make a reason on why John was acting like a boy. Several time she kept thinking that John were so inconsiderate, inconsistent and so childish.

He seemed that nothing bothered him. She tried all kind of way to adapt to his non sense buy she was going more and more out of her mind.

★ ★ ★

I did warned her about John, I said he were a narcissist! John is so immature, a two years old will look like a grandpa next to him.

Michelle ended up going to depression and she attempted suicide. Eventually she turned into recreational drugs to deal with John's games.

It didn't have to end that way, it didn't have to even start, if she only could have seen the red flags

★ ★ ★

C H A P T E R

Reason #4 Co-occurring Issues

The W.A.S in this scenario may have an ongoing problem with alcohol and/or drugs that affects his decision-making.

We will use a substance addiction in that case but could be a video game addiction or gambling or shopping.

* * *

Keep adding any addiction you can think of or have sadly been aware of.

Those addictions do create serious issues with Co-occurring behaviors resulting in regrettable sexual decisions.

A few less cases but with a major aftermath issues are simply those linked to a sexual addiction.

A W.A.S with a sexual addiction will show a pattern of behaviors leading to an excessive amount of sexual connections.

Easily say, the W.A.S will compulsively engage in sexual fantasies and/ or behaviors as a way to numb out and avoid life realities.

Allo?

Good morning, sorry to wake you up, you have an appointment in our clinic tomorrow at 8am so we are calling to confirm that you are still coming?

Yes I will and it's ok

Jamila hung up the phone and decided to get up after all, she does have a full day at a job she dislikes more than anything.

It's so frustrating to work at a company where you are not appreciated. Her feelings got worse since they fired Keisha for being sick smh I hope she sued them saying it out loud. After a long inhalation she stretched her slender sexy body and was ready for the day.

Jamila took an unnecessary long shower and lathered her body with so much attention that it looked like she was being filmed for an advertisement. She decided to wear all pink for the day to put some joy in her heart. Her car was parked near the entry of her condo so since she didn't have to take a long walk she will simply wear them heels to match that Pamela Anderson's look she believed she created today.

Jamila was a fine Arabic princess, looking like she just came out of a cartoon show. She was milky brown with some plump pink lips, she was shaped like a Spanish guitar and her skin was like a baby velvet touch. She seemed to make any perfume chemically turned into an arousal substance once they mixed with her scents. Jamila was also funny, smart, soft spoken and always smiling. Let me tell you about her diamond sparkling white looking teeth! Was she made in Heaven or what???

Jamila probably created more traffic jams than a construction road. She was simply an amazing creature, almost an alien but she was human with feeling and after Joshua she was no longer the same.

Let's talk about that psycho addicted perver while we are on the subject. Joshua was this handsome dark skinned intelligent brother born with a verb on his tongue. He was in denial of his drinking problem and thought he was in control. Of course he was not! Joshua lost a great opportunity to succeed beyond belief because of his alcohol intake but surely he blamed the fact that he was a black man.

Joshua was raised by a single mother and his dad was never in the picture. He never mentioned either of them since his mom's passing.

His uncle Josh was the person that helped Joshua finish college and find his internship where he was able to flourish successfully as he did.

The firm that hired him wanted to make him a partner but the last office party was decisive in a negative input from the other partners. Joshua drank so much he ended up in underwear and tie. If you see the picture I am too embarrassed to give more details.

Joshua was a darn good lawyer but the alcohol party after each win was too much for anyone to give him more responsibilities or wanted him to be any representation.

Now I am sure you all are wondering how Jamila and Joshua met and what happened right?

So Jamila hired Joshua to represent her divorce case pretty much you all know, they won't be the case, Jamila ended up with a nice financial compensation from her ex for cheating on her with his administrative assistant and having a baby with her.

Joshua and Jamila ended up in a bar after court to celebrate. Long story short they woke up in a motel 6 both naked so we assumed they had a fun night.

Jamila was going to the clinic for an abortion resulting from that night entirely full of bad decisions.

Joshua was not aware of her being pregnant nor getting an abortion.

Jamila went through the process, aborted the result of a drunk night as she named that episode of her life. She blocked Joshua's phone number. She moved to Atlanta from Washington State and got ready for a new chapter with that annoying job she kept since she simply transferred location.

Joshua used to one night stand so at first he was ok not to see her again but when he realized she blocked his number, his man's ego took the control of his brain. He needed to see her again, what happened to women calling him back and begging to see him again? This Jamila was an enigma, does she think she can get rid of him just like that?

Joshua started to focus more and more on Jamila and decided to hire a private Investigator to find her. Not even 24hours John Cartigo the Investigator he hired found his Arabe Princess in a little town in Georgia about 30 minutes from Atlanta.

Joshua took a leave of 2 weeks and headed to Jamila without any real plan in mind, he was convinced that's the woman of his life.

Joshua stopped by a jewelleries store in the airport on his way out and purchased a $10k diamond ring surrounded by sapphires. When the sales person asked him the size he smiled and said it doesn't matter if it doesn't fit we will make some adjustments.

He was impressed by his boldness, never he thought he would get married, nevertheless that Joshua will be chasing a woman he barely knows, a former client that blocked him after a drunk Night sleep on the other side of the country. He was smiling just thinking about it.

Exactly 2 hours after landing he was parked outside of her work place, he knew where she lives but he didn't want to scare her.

Jamila had just moved to that beautiful city and she decided to head to the furniture store downtown before heading home. She was extremely surprised to hear her name yelled pretty loudly by her voice she swore she recognized. She froze and refused to look in the direction of the sound. She could hear the steps getting closer and closer.

"Jamila" … she turned around and saw him even more sexy that she can remember with the cologne feeling her nostrils already.

"Joshua" said as naturally as she could.

"Jamila, I am sorry for showing up on you like that", he grabbed both of her hands as if she could run away again from him.

She could barely speak so she chose to be quiet and plastered a smile on her face with her eyebrows showing that she was intrigued.

"Jamila, I can't stop thinking of you, I tried to move on but I can't. I can't work. I can't eat, I can't sleep, all I think about it's you. I miss you, I wanted to see you again. Will you please give me 5 minutes of your time? I just want a chance to show you that it can be us".

Jamila was already turned up by his boldness, she was touched and intrigued.

She agreed to go to the coffee spot next to her office.

Joshua was walking so close to her and never let her hand go like she would have run away as soon as she was free.

They sat and started to talk as if they never departed from each other. Joshua asked her about this new location, the city and the food spots around. She asked him about his recent cases and his tennis partners as well as his dog Sultan. They laughed, got closer and ended up at her house making up again.

This time Joshua knew he cannot live without Jamila, he needs that in his life. The only way he can keep going will be with her.

He woke up earlier than Jamila, ordered breakfast, and hid the ring in the orange juice glass.

Jamila almost swallowed the ring! Thank God she choked that out and said yes with tears.

They got married in Vegas a week later and friends and family were so surprised on both sides. They never heard of either and couldn't believe Jamila got remarried so soon and Joshua, this bachelor for life, was hooked out of nowhere.

Joshua even stopped drinking and seemed to have found his balance.

No one was surprised this time when 10 months later Jamila gave birth to a boy named Joshua Jr, he was the spit image of his dad.

Joshua Jr was bored with serious issues and ended up dying 3 weeks later.

It was very hard for both of them. Jamila fell into depression, feeling guilty. Thinking she was being punished from the abortion. She came clean to Joshua who chose to end in a bar, started drinking again and flirting. Not even a week after the confession of Jamila, Joshua was cheating on her with an ex booty call. Then it returned to drinking every night and cheating.

Jamila didn't know what to do. She believed she deserved it.

No one deserves to be cheated on. No one should blame alcohol for a decision they choose to make.

Joshua has not matured in life. He reacted to an Impulse mostly because this man lacked control and discipline.

Jamila knew that Joshua was spontaneous, bold and made impulsive decisions.

Joshua is a W.A.S a dependency to alcohol not a good combination.

Jamila lied, killed Joshua's prior unborn child without his knowledge. She failed him!

CHAPTER

Five

Reason #5 Selfishness

It is absolutely possible the W.A.S primary consideration is for themselves and themselves alone.

They could therefore lie and keep secrets without any sort of remorse or regret.

For the W.A.S what is important is to get what they want.

It's possible that the W.A.S never intended to be monogamous from the beginning of the relationship.

The W.A.S could have been honest at the beginning of the relationship about their real intentions.

Instead, they lied and played along with the other partners intentions.

This W.A.S will be the one that will never volunteer to tell you anything about their intentions but mimic your words.

A selfish W.A.S already has an agenda which they have never intended to modify.

Their partner will be misled to believe that their lack of sharing their intentions are results of trust issues from their past.

Every person in this world has an intention whether they share it or not in the beginning of any relationship.

Some are an open book, others are a mysterious book and more are a close book.

What is in their book will reveal their intention, personality and the outcome of your relationship with them.

Red flags are great indicators of what is in those books. Just trust your instincts since you are not a mind reader.

Julie, Florian saw your husband dropped you at the maternity ward, is it some I should know?

Debra was looking at me with the ugly winks she displayed from time to time when she thinks we are that cool.

I bursted into the loudest laugh I could make and replied, "Girl, what kind of drug your son is taking because God knows, no way I am not even near been pregnant, we are still trying"

"Wow I am sorry Julie, I thought you finally got pregnant!"

"It's ok lady, it will happen in due time"

When Debra left, I hurried to call my hubby, as usual he answered on the 2nd ring but stayed very quiet after I finished my story. That was not unusual for him since I am the most talkative in our marriage but for some unknown reason I felt a chill coming down my back. I probably was getting sick or some.

"OK Honey, I see you tonight" he finally said

"I love you"

"Love you too" he replied and hung up.

The rest of the day I couldn't shake that uneasy feeling that was crawling in my back.

I decided to paint a little to spend time while waiting on my hubby love.

We have been married for five years now and still have no baby. I know Jonathan wants a boy to carry his name. His family is also on my back on that note, I need to call back his mom.

This middle-aged woman that looks like a teenager always made me jealous of her body lines. She looks so perfect ahiii I always wondered if she could be a vampire of some sort.

"Hi Mother"

"Hello my sweet sweet daughter in love, what good news do you have for me"

"Mother just the humble me, missing you"

Mrs Jones always knew how to make me feel good and bad at the same time.

I knew she was referring to me been pregnant yet

After chatting with her for about 30 minutes, mostly about her daughter Sophie and her upcoming wedding, I decided to take a bath to relax a little before Jonathan gets home. We are going on our weekly date night.

My life with Jonathan was very simple. We were successful in our businesses, he owned a company of landscapes that was also handling snow removal during the winter so his business was making money all year round. My neighbors was so envious of our front and back yard that Jonathan was constantly upgrading and using as portfolio for his A plus clients as he named the very rich ones

My cleaning business was also doing well. I started by babysitting when I was twelve then cleaned around and made it my mission to sparkle every home I used to babysit.

Then a few clients were actually calling me more for the cleaning than the babysitter. Today after 20 years, I now turned my business into a franchise in all fifty states and making a million dollars a year.

I met Jonathan when I was cleaning fifteen years ago on this contract I had for Judge Butler, he was responsible for the landscape. He gave me a ride and kept giving me a ride. We started dating a year after and move together ten years ago. It was hard to get married because Jonathan wanted me to get pregnant before he proposed and I didn't want to have a baby without been married. I finally won, we got married but I am still not pregnant

I was so afraid that Jonathan gets tired of me.

Our life was peaceful until the day of April first 2011 when I received a call from a woman named Shawn. She wanted to talk to me and asked me to meet her in the lobby of Hotel Roses.

I talked to Jonathan about it and thought it was strange and I wasn't sure it was concerning a contract. He just looked at me for a very long time and kiss me on the forehead while holding me for a very long time.

I was very uneasy but I went to meet this strange lady since no one but me seemed to make a big deal of it.

She told me she will be wearing a black dress with a blue flower in her hair.

That will not be a mystery for too long since I am at the hotel lobby now.

It was only one lady sitting in a corner of the bar dining area.

She vaguely favours me and she didnt looked weird from a distance. She was busy looking at her purse or some next to her. I quietly approached her.

"Shawn?"

She turned and smiled at me as if she knew me.

That crazy feeling again went down my back

"HI Julie, thank you for accepting to meet me"

I still was looking very puzzled with a millions of questions.

"Please have a seat, I will explain everything to you"

I guess she saw my face.

I pulled a chair across from her and realized that she was sitting next to a carseat.

"OH, you have a baby in that thing? How precious!"

She looked at the baby then blushed and almost right away waived at the server.

"How can I help you ladies?"

"Julie, what do you want to drink?"

The way she was saying my name as if she truly knew me made me want to smack her but I smiled and said the strongest drink you have.

The server winked and agreed and left.

"OK Shawn, I believe it's your name?" And without letting her confirm, I continue "what is it that you want to talk to me about? Must be important for you to bring your newborn here"

Without blanking she looks at me straight in the eyes and said "this is Jonathan's son"

Thanks God, my drink has just arrived and I swallowed the entire content of with no doubt the most strongest crap I ever tasted.

"More of this please" I asked the server that was looking at me with his eyes wide open. Probably no more wink for me from him.

A burst of despair grew into my heart and it felt so suffocating that I passed out.

"Hello, Julie?"

All I could see was this blue flower and I remembered everything.

A river of tears was coming out of my eyes and I couldn't help the feeling of weakness.

I was in total despair, lost, what just happened.

Jonathan seemed more busy lately

Busy with what? Making babies?

How did Jonathan and I end up like this?

He once said that I meant the world to him.

However, he already fell in love with someone else within three years of their marriage. She wondered if he was finally revealing his trueself.

The reality that Jonathan was not only cheating on her and even made a child with that Shawn finally began to sink in her brain.

"I will be right to say my time as a fruitless tree is now over".

Three years later.

Men were the most cruel creatures in the world and Jonathan was one of the leaders of the pack.

How selfish can he be? Like I never wanted to have kids.

I went through a series of testing, treatments, put on extra weight all this to end with Shawn's baby.

He was a coward as well.

He couldn't even tell me that.

He sent his mistress to be their little bastard.

Why Jonathan, why?

After all we did together? I gave you my virginity, I gave you loyalty, are we financially stable?

I thought we were in Love...

Why Jonathan why?

CHAPTER

Six

Reason #6: Anger/Revenge

The W.A.S may cheat to get revenge.

They may be angry with their mate so the goal is to hurt them.

In such cases, the infidelity is meant to be seen and known.

The W.A.S does not bother to lie or keep secrets about their cheating, because he wants his partner to know about it.

They brag about it out loud.

Anger or revenge are strange behaviors which only make sense in the mind of the one demonstrating it.

In those cases "sorry" won't be enough, making their favorite meal or giving them a blow job won't fix it.

The W.A.S may or may not warn you it's up to how dysfunctional their mind will be.

The main goal is for them to feel like they inflicted the same amount of pain if not more that they felt.

Those cases are personality based.

The kind of you get what you pay for or what goes around comes back around.

Regardless if the W.A.S was hurt intentionally or not, the revenge will be intentional and the Anger is absolutely real.

They feel hurt and betrayed so they retaliate. Just that simple!

Staring at Bruce and Sophia but I still can't believe it. Why will he want me to see that?

I understand we may not have a great relationship since I was promoted to Vice Regional President of the Company.

Bruce has been nothing but rude to me.

Tonight he invited me to meet him at the Five Resorts where we went for our honeymoon.

A black rose, a card with a room number and a note saying "better or worse".

I would have never guessed that I would have been dressed up in a pretty black dress, my finest lingerie and his favorite heels ...looking at my husband and my best friend.

How did we get here?

"Bruce, what is going on?"

"What do you mean? Are you blind?"

While Sophia desperately was working on covering herself, Bruce was laying proud and naked with an arrogant smirk on his face.

"Why Sophia"? I asked

"Why not Sophia?" "You want to be a man right, you want to compete with me right, you think you control everything right? You should focus on your marriage as you focus on your job! Your out of measure ambition did that to you! So ask yourself why? Don't ask me.

Now you can join us or get the f★★k out of here!

He then pulled Sophia that was so lost and proceeded to kiss her.

At that moment, my brain was totally numb. Bruce, my hubby as I used to familiarly call him, just betrayed me. Not only he cheated on me but as a psychopath that he wanted me to witness it.

How disrespectful can he be? And Sophia, smh Sophia, I don't even want to think about her.

What should I do? How did we get there?

We swore to have each other back, now he betrayed me. We promised to be millionaires before we turn 40 years old and now we are only 38 years old, he betrayed me.

"Wow Bruce how could you?"

I couldn't even find the right questions to ask.

Almost if I knew he would one day but why was I with him?

We met in High school and we have been together for 20 years now.

Are we done? How can we overcome that betrayal?

The tears were rushing on my face, my knees were clutching on each other... for the first time in my life I was weak, I was empty, drained and absolutely powerless.

All I did was for us, I was faithful to our promises, our plans, our dreams.

I love my Hubby, I love him from all my heart.

I rejected so many offers for him and now here we are, I am done.

What can I do? I don't even know how to reach him anymore, I feel like this is not my hubby.

Bruce is gone!

From my opinion: This is not a lost relationship, Bruce is not gone and can be regained back. The issue with Bruce was concerning his self esteem as a Man! His wife was a self accomplished Lady who understood the assignment, the promises since High school. Bruce as a typical W.A.S got distracted, lost in life and forgot the mutual goal. No Sophia doesn't need Bruce but why not keep the marriage after all it was 20 years invested. Sophia is a Leader, An accomplished lady, she can easily bounce back, right now she is hurt. Bruce needs reassurance, he needs to know that he has control. He is scared to lose his woman, she is no longer the shy high school girl. She is a Boss Lady and he is scared, she is transforming into a powerful lady making him realize that he is way behind her and he is not up to the challenge. Sophia can be more submissive by sharing her moves with him and give him the impressions that his opinion is considered. She can play the game as many women are doing to keep a partner not at their level of achievement but a partner who can bring them stability and help them stay humble. Any successful woman could use a Bruce.

CHAPTER

Seven

Reason #7: Insecurity

The W.A.S may feel as complex as complex can be.

When they are not young enough this is the problem or too young.

Not cute or not handsome enough.

Not rich or successful enough.

No college Diploma so not smart enough, etc. An astonishing amount of W.A.S cheating is linked, at least in part, to a mid-life crisis.

Therefore to bolster their flagging ego, they will be seeking validation from others rather than their mate.

Their beliefs are based on the fact that perhaps, this sextracurricular spark of interest to feel wanted, desired, and worthy **will be fulfilled by a new partner.**

Possibly the first spark can be recreated.

When I met Mohamed He was very shy and so insecure.

We met through mutual friends at her party where I was supposed to be matched with his friend.

He was just there, not drinking or smoking like everyone else at the table.

We all were joking, laughing as hard as we could but Mohamed was just quiet. From time to time I can see that he was looking at me from the corner of his eyes and will shy away as soon as I try to capture his look.

Mohamed got me inquisitive that night and I remember our 1st meeting as if it was today when it's actually been over 30 years.

Time flies, that's all I can say.

The next day I decided to get more information about him so I asked my date whom I didn't really like, well he was a thief or like they said a cleptoman. He stole my necklace that night.

That loser was not trying to give me any information on Mohamed, telling me, he is not like us, he is not open mind, he is a real Muslim, his family is very traditional.

The more he was working on convincing me to stop wondering about Mohamed, the more I wanted to know about him.

I remembered they said he owned a store on Main Street, selling electronics well, let me look for it.

About a week later, I was ready to hunt for my man. I had just received my new outfit and boy let me tell you. That outfit was on fire!

Put on my new perfume from Oscar De La Renta, smelling like an Angel going to church.

My plan was simple, first drive on Main Street and locate an electronics store then accidentally walk unto him, hopefully it was there today because I didn't want that outfit to go to waste.

I started to get discouraged, Main Street was actually a long street when you are looking for a specific location. A few cars beeping their stupid horns for no reason, all I can think of was the face of Mohamed.

Will he recognize me, we only met one time at night. Is he really a serious Muslim? Is his family that traditional? Why will he be that traditional but hanging out in the bar with people like us, I mean me? Yes he didn't drink that night nor smoke cigarettes or drugs but he was there, very comfy.

In the midst of all my thousand questions, I couldn't believe my eyes. I found his store and it had to be his store because I could read Mohamed Electronics. That dude was too simple. While I was laughing out loud, I started to also build anxiety. The plan was smart, easy, manipulative. I can do it. I keep telling myself, I can do it. I can do all I put my mind to and I am strong, I am beautiful, I got this.

I parked right in front so he could see me coming out of my Ford Mustang GT flashy red.

A deep head turned in my direction and I knew it was all because I looked good.

Someone held the door open as I walked up the 2 little steps.

I acted like I was looking for a TV, they said a new kind of TV was coming out with a remote control so I had to have it.

They called the boss because I sound like a client that has money to spend and wants a new arrival or future arrival.

I knew Mohamed was coming behind me, I could feel my hair rising on my back and my inner thighs getting warmer and wetter.

Why did I have such a crazy attraction for a dude that never even talked to me?

I heard excuse me, do you need help.

I slowly turned around and I proceeded to request the TV then stopped myself mid sentence and said: hey ... I remember you!

He smiled and blushed right there in front of me!

I couldn't believe my eyes, is that guy having a crush on me?

Yes it's me I guessed, I remember you as well.

We locked eyes for the first time and I knew this guy was mine forever.

He has green eyes, I couldn't see all that the first night. He also has dimples, coming God, what are you doing?

I smiled as hard as I could to show him how glad I was to see him again.

Strangely, he was talking to me normally, no longer shy and that turned me on even more. How many levels of turned on can a person have? This guy is crawling on my skin with his eyes. He looked so curious. Like he wanted to know me, taking my clothes off with his eyes, he was making me feel naked and vulnerable.

I was taken by his eyes, I was under his absolute control.

Yes I did order the TV, yes we set up a time to have a drink when I knew he was not a drinker.

Mohamed did even drink coffee, what a guy.

Long story short. We started to date, we made love every night at my house, passionate love.

Every morning at 3am, Mohamed was leaving my house with the pretext that he needed to be home to pray by 4am.

I hated missing him so much. I wanted to wake up with him looking at the sun.

Mohamed took me to his private home by the beach one weekend and he took me into his arms to watch the sun awakening together.

Mohamed answered all my complaints by fixing it, making it happen.

We have been dating for one year and we slept together every night until 3am since our first night.

I wanted more out of our relationship. I was feeling insecure because I loved him so much and I was wondering why he was hiding me.

The others didn't know we were dating, no one in his family knew we were dating, only him and me knew. He said to me he was a very private person and didn't want anyone in his business.

I used to cry every night after year 2. He gave me a beautiful watch full of diamonds with a perfect cut. I was spoiled, he was now paying my rent, my car note, everything I ever wanted. He was giving me a weekly allowance. I was no longer working. I was living my life just waiting for my man to come home so I could feed him food and my body. Mohamed knew how to eat me. Mohamed was the only man that could make an oasis at each part of my body he touches. His hands were soft and he was constantly caressing me. Playing with me. My entire skin was not a secret for Mohamed. He knew each square millimeter of me. I exploded in his mouth more times than anyone else I ever dated combined. Mohamed was an expert in body pleasure.

Year 3, Mohamed was still keeping our relationship a secret, he was still leaving me at 3pm but at least now we were at the Beach house every weekend.

Year 5, avec many nights of tears, thousands of gifts, our relationship now turned abusive. Mohamed choked me a few times, kicked me in the stomach and for my birthday I had a black eyes and a new car; go figure.

I feel like less than me, Mohamed is still coming home every night, now his friends know we are dating but his family still doesn't know.

I want to get married but Mohamed said he can't because his family already chose his bride. He said he will never defy his family but I can remain second in his life. He said he will buy me a house and will help me own a business if I am bored. He said he wants kids and he knows I can't give him a baby. I wanted us to use a surrogate using his sperm but he refused.

Mohamed got me to question myself.

Joe approached me and told me that he noticed that I am not looking happy as I used to. I needed a friend to talk to.

Mohamed had to travel to meet his future wife.

I was devastated, Joe took me out for a drink and we ended up sleeping together.

Maybe I was drunk but I didn't like it like with Mohamed. Mohamed was made for me but I was scared, I was pushing him away with arguments, I couldn't help myself.

Joe was so sweet on the other hand, he told me he would not treat me like Mohamed treated me, he would not be ashamed of me, he would stand up to his family for me. Joe said I was amazing, Joe said I was beautiful, Joe said he loves me.

Mohamed never said he loves me, Mohamed never said I was beautiful, Mohamed never said he loves me.

The more I compared those two men, the more I was troubled, the more Mohamed and I argued.

That terrible day happened, Joe came for lunch since Mohamed didn't come until 7pm.

We were naked having lunch. I heard a door knob turn but it was too late to move or do anything. Joe face was so white like he saw a ghost and I had to match that skin tone as soon as my eyes locked Mohamed's.

Mohamed's eyes penetrated my soul, I felt ashamed, I swore I felt like Judas when he betrayed Jesus.

Mohamed stood at the door. Looking at me as if he never saw me before. Joe was gathering his clothes and apologizing. I was sitting on the sofa, and didn't know what my next move. I knew it was over, I knew I messed up a good relationship because I was insecure buy mostly stupid.

Mohamed asked me one question after Joe left.

Why Michael, why?

I don't know Mohamed, I am sorry. We have been together for so long, I love you, I submitted to you, my entire life revolved around you but you didn't and never gave me a fair chance in our relationship.

Michael, do you understand that I am a Muslim, I will be destroy by my family if they know you are a Man, you can't gave me a kid, from day one I told you that we will never get married and this will be just that but I will love and spoil you and I showed you, so why now, why Joe, why Michael, why?

CHAPTER

Eight

Reason #8: Unrealistic Expectations

The W.A.S may feel that their partner should meet their every whim of sexual desire 24/7.

Regardless of how they feel or what is going on at any particular moment.

The W.A.S will fail to understand that their partners have a life of their own.

Perhaps also thoughts, feelings and needs that don't always involve them.

When their expectations are not met, they will seek external fulfillment.

Just as simple as this.

Depending on the partner they will cheat with, it can get as vicious as vicious can get.

I am 22 years old, I live with my older sister. She is 38. She takes extremely good care of me, and paid for my college tuition so I don't have to get a part time job. She also gives me enough stipend money to cover all my other needs. She also surprises me from time to time with a trip or extra cash or expensive purse.

My sister, whose name I will change for the purpose of privacy, let's call her G. She never was able to have a kid and treated me like the daughter she never had.

Her hubby Joshua lives with us in a 3 bedroom mansion.

It turns out that Josh and I ended up sleeping together.

Up to now, I still couldn't explain how this happened.

He is so charming, loving, caring, with my sister and me.

The man is like a God, Adonis, so freaking sexy.

His gaze turns my head, I don't know how to say no to him.

Some girls who read this might understand this feeling. I'm ashamed of what I did but I don't know who to confide in and sadly it's hard to even feel a genuine regretful feeling.

Eventually I couldn't control my feelings any longer, I was tired of fantasizing about him at night, playing with myself watching this pic he took when he graduated college. Well, I ended up confessing to him that I have feelings more than brother in law type of feelings. To my great surprise Josh too made it clear to me that he felt the same for me but that he didn't want to hurt my sister because she is a wonderful woman but she is so boring in bed. He doesn't think she is sexy like me. He felt like they grew apart but she is such an amazing caregiver. She works a lot, take care of everything for us. G planned our dinners menu, our vacations, the cleaning schedule, the house decorations, the family in law Christmas and birthday gifts. She is so multi-task, his family adore her.

We flirted several times.

When my sister is away, he and I behave like a real couple.

I am young with a beautiful body, I am home more than my sister so I am sexually available when and where. It's not a place in the house we haven't made love in.

Josh think I am more flexible than sister and he called my tities the defend fruits. Josh is so funny, we laugh so much together but with my sister they are so cordial, polite, boring.

He makes love to me like no one has ever done to me.

He also says he feels amazing with me.

We became very much in love with each other.

So! We both went deep in our feelings and a few times we almost got caught but G is so naive she probably can't believe we can do this. She thought we were doing yoga smh

Now I want him to divorce my sister so that we can live alone and our relationship can become official.

I may be cruel, but I just can't stand seeing them together, kissing in front of me and it drives me crazy! I wished he would file for a divorce, he said he wants it and would like it too, but it needs to be done gently so as not to hurt my sister. For now, he suggests that I go and rent a house somewhere else and that he will come by often.

Anyway I am pregnant and that will do.

CHAPTER

Nine

Reason #9: It's over version 1

The W.A.S may want to end their current relationship.

However, instead of just telling their partner that they are unhappy.

The W.A.S simply want to break things off by cheating — and then force their partner to do the dirty work.

Those cases will mostly involve emotional and physical cheating.

All weapons are used by the W.A.S to regain their freedom out of their relationship.

It's Over, Version 2

The W.A.S may want to end their current relationship, but not until they got another one lined up.

So they set the stage for their next relationship while still in the first one.

Those behavior can be seen as a cheating behavior regardless it involves a sexual contact or not.

The act of engaging with expectation of finding a replacement itself is a cheating act.

The intention is as bad as the action.

At approximately 4:45pm on February 14, 2014, Chantal, my best friend since kindergarten, poked her head around my cubicle wall and said, "More Lovers are getting married today so we are staying open till we are done."

"What?"

"More Lovers are getting so we are mandatory till we are done"

"What?!?"

"LOVERS! ARE GETTING MARRIED! NO HOME UNTIL DONE!"

"For real? Today? WHY?"

"Yes, for real. Thought you might want to know it's Valentine's Day!."

I walked out of my cubby and looked across the hall toward the County Clerk's Office. Sure enough, there were still over 20 couples standing in line outside the door.

I stared.

"Is this really happening?" I thought.

I went back to my desk and pulled up my phone. Indeed it was Valentine's Day. How did I miss that?

At 4:50pm, I texted Sharon, who was tied up in her office as well after a court case needed to finish her report.

"We should get married today, Lovers are getting married today and we are open until they are done and it's still almost 20 couples in line, enough time for you to get here"

She wrote back: "??????"

Then: "Hold on...what?????"

"I guess so... Lovers are getting married across from my office right now and it's Valentine's Day."

I went back into the hall. Though it had only been twenty minutes, there were now around 15 couples in line outside the clerk's office.

In addition to the line of couples waiting, excited friends and family of those with newly issued marriage licenses began to crowd around most couples as they exited the clerk's office. Each group of excited people moved to an area of the second floor that still had some space. Every 10 minutes, there would be cheering from a different area of the hall as one couple after another got married. The feeling of Love was everywhere and pure joy, on repeat, throughout the building.

I called Sharon since she still hasn't responded to my text: "You should come to my office on your way home from work. Lovers are getting married and it's AWESOME to witness."

I watched around 10 couples get married, and by then she still was not here yet.

I was now wondering, were we a couple? Or a Loving couple or were we lovers? We talked about marriage, kids, we have been living together for about 3 years now but are we ready to get married?

It was now almost 8pm and only 2 couples remained.

Sharon texted me informing me that she was parking and heading my way.

I hurried back to my office and printed a packet of marriage license applications, then I grabbed a clipboard and two pens.

I also took the gift I purchased for Sharon for Valentine's Day.

Then I stood in line and started filling out our application. When Sharon arrived I just handed her the clipboard and asked her to sign and to give me her driver license as required on the license.

Part of my brain started to panic. What if Sharon was not ready? Nothing she said confirmed that we were on the same page.What if this was actually the end of our relationship? Was this about to close our chapter? How would I take the rejection? I do love her and I am sure she is the one but was she sure about me? I should ask her! Right now! Yes! But I'd heard people get rejected on Valentine's day as well.

All these thoughts were spinning in my head, but I never turned any of them into actual words. Instead, I looked down at the applications still on the clipboard in my hand. Then I turned to Sharon and said, "HERE! Sign here!"

Sharon was looking at me and I keep avoiding eye contact.

"Was that a proposal?" She asked

"I don't know," then I grabbed her applications and handed both to the employee thanking him for staying after hours for us all, and she smiled sincerely and said, "We're so happy to be here to do this for you. Let me take this to my computer to enter it and I'll be right back."

After she left us alone at the counter, Sharon turned to me, eyebrows raised, and said, "ARE WE GOING TO TALK ABOUT THIS?!?"

I pulled out of my pocket a little package that I opened and showed her a ring box holding two rings.

"I was going to give this to you for Valentine'sDay dinner tonight," I said as I pulled the ring out of the box. "But today's events bumped up my timeline by a couple hours. I knew since the first day I met you that I wanted to marry you.. I knew you were the one for me since you look at me with your pretty brown eyes.You are more than anything I ever dreamed of Sharon. So... will you marry me?"

Sharon's jaw dropped, and she was lucky for me and our relationship said yes. Honestly, I'm not entirely sure she would have said yes if I hadn't had the rings. They let her know I wasn't just asking to take advantage of the romantic euphoria. She realized I'd genuinely wanted this before all this fever, and she saw that I'd made plans to ask her regardless of any cute date in the calendar or the media's coverage I forgot to mention.

When we left the clerk's office with that precious marriage license, we ran into more friends and loved ones in the hall, including our close friends, Chantal who worked with me and Mike that I texted optimistically, also a minister neighbor who was offered her services a year after I met Sharon. Chantal and Mike agreed to be our witnesses, and Reverend Peters performed the ceremony.

We have been married for four years now and I caught Sharon cheated on me twice already. She seemed regretful but not quite sincerely sorry.

I keep wondering where I went wrong. Did I change? Am I no longer the same person she married or felt in love with?

I was there when she transitioned and regardless of what my family said, I actually cut them all off just for her.

My mother was mortified knowing we may never have our own kids but I told her we could adopt.

Was it maybe the side effect of all those hormones? Maybe I couldn't satisfy her enough.

"Sharon, we need to talk"

"About???"

"Sweety you cheated again on me"

"OH that!"

I was about to lose my temper but I needed to stay calm because I may not be able to handle if she says she doesn't want this marriage any longer

"Sharon, what can I do to make you happy, loyal?"

She took a long breathe, look at me in the eyes

"Are you bothered by me sleeping with other people?"

"Sharon…"

"Just answer the damn question Nicholas, it's always Sharon this, Sharon that, all I want to know is are you bothered with me sleeping with other people?"

She yelled at me again, always yelled at me when she is confronted, not sure if I can support anymore of that but to may surprise I quietly answered

"No sweety, I get a little jealous but as long as you are happy that's what matters to me"

She smiled, grab my face and kiss me

"I am late for work so make sure you put our reservation for dinner tonight, I don't feel like cooking"

She left the room only her spicy perfume reminded me of her past presence.

Was I ready to have her leave me?

I was upset inside because I showed all the love possible to Sharon even when she was Seth. I was there during her surgeries, her multiple treatments to achieve her total transformation. I paid most of them before our insurance covered the rest. Now she is very beautiful, sexy and so adorable unless she is confronted.

She told me I can leave if I am not happy and go where? I don't want to Start another relationship. After all, I invested in her.

She just wants me to say goodbye but I am not going to. I am laughed at by females about me dating a fake woman and still being cheated on. I am laugh by men calling me gay. My own mom won't look me in the eyes. I can't leave Sharon, I do love her, she is special and she's been through so much. I want to stay and work on our issues, after all isn't what marriage is about and I am not a quitter.

CHAPTER

Ten

Reason #10: Childhood Abuse

The W.A.S may be reenacting or latently responding to unresolved childhood trauma — neglect, emotional abuse, physical abuse, sexual abuse, etc.

In such cases, their childhood wounds have created attachment/intimacy issues that leave them unable or unwilling to fully commit to one person.

They might also be using the excitement and distraction of sexual infidelity as a way to self-soothe the pain of these old, unhealed wounds.

When I met Mike he was a total mess! I mean the guy was a loser!

Mike used to sleep where the night found him and woke up in a different bed every morning.

I just got my divorce so he was exactly what I needed, no commitment, no promises, no lies, all fun and no tomorrow.

Mike used all kinds of drugs, drank all type of liquors and smoked whatever brand of cigarette he could borrow.

I used to ask myself how this dude can even function.

We were invited in a gay bar one evening and Mike made out with a dude, like straight made out with a dude. We were all drunk and ended up with a 3 some with that dude which of course was not interested in me but I got a fee spanks on my butt.

Mike was so free in his attitude, always smiling, laughing. He was so happy.

I love to spend time with Mike because he never questioned anything. No pressure, the guy was the coolest ever.

He started to cancel a few of his other thousand dates to hang out with me. He used to call me buddy and I love that name. Not a baby, not a sweetheart, my pet name was buddy.

Mike knew a lot of people, he was social, friendly, blunt but I think his laugh was what charmed everyone around him. Mike laughed like it was no tomorrow.

I also love his stature, he was athletic looking with this black Ebony shiny skin complexion.

Mike also has those straight teeth you only see after a photoshop. His smile has nothing to do with being jealous of the sun. Mike was my best friend, my buddy.

He was a freak, a comedian, reckless, the most honest man I ever met.

Eventually I started to fall in love with my Buddy and I started to envy those other girls or men rubbing on his body.

I was missing him when he was not near me. I used to sleep on his pillows when he left for work in the morning.

I planned a trip to the DR with Mike and I wanted him away from everyone so I can charm him and maybe make him exclusive.

In the plane Mike was flirting with this beautiful flight attendant, while we had more drinks than we deserve he got her number and I got jealous.

I was feeling Mike more than I wanted to but my excuse was that we were buddies for 5 years now so when that stopped.

In the Dr while the sun and the breeze made our stay so romantic, Mike was romantic all right with half of the women in the resort.

The last night after sharing my bed with numerous unknown whores I felt that it was time for Mike and me to have a conversation.

"Mike, we need to talk"

The way he looks at me, confirmed that he understood the seriousness of the request.

"Buddy, is everything OK? He asked me

"Yes but Mike, I have been your loyal buddy for 5 years and all you do is still enjoying others, will that ever be going to change? Are you ever going to be exclusive?"

Mike took a long 3 minutes, looking me in the eyes as he could read my mind. His face changed so many times, it seemed like thousands of emotions were passing through.

"Buddy, I love you, I love you more than you think, I love you more than I ever loved anyone, I love you more than myself"

So why can't we be exclusive Mike? Why do you need all those strangers in our bed, why do you still sleep with Monica, Adele and Rhonda?"

"Buddy, trust me those people mean nothing to me. Buddy they are a sex toys, some that make me happy that keeps me happy. I will not be the same Buddy if I cut them off. I can't face Buddy…"

Mike put his head down so I walked up to him and lifted his head. To my huge surprise, Mike was crying, tears flowing out of his eyes so abundantly that it scared me.

"Mike, what's going on? You scare me"

He held me tight in his arms kiss my forehead and told me the worst real life story I ever heard.

"Buddy, I lost my virginity to my Dad when I was 5, he told me Mickey, sex is not that serious, I eill never hurt you because you are my boy but I will show you stuff so you will be the best at this and you can control anybody, you will be the King. My day called me King Meek since that day. When I was about 10 he introduced me to my first woman and that was my mother, he told me after he opened my mom leg ...this is where you came out so you King Meek will go back in and come out renew. My mom was a Crack addicted, she did everything my dad asked her to do. She slept for the rent, for the cable to stay on, with thr mechanic so Daddy'car can be fixed when needed. Mommy was devoted to my Dad.

I grew up drinking, fucking, been fucked, drugged and smoked in and out.

I am no good for anyone. I realized when I went to high school that apparently I was abused by my parents, simply because no other kids has the same experience. I had to choose be King Meek or face my abuse and go in therapy like a wimp or a loser like my Dad told me when I confronted him. I choose to be King Meek Buddy, that's all I know how to be. I met you and you are so sweet, you are just a good woman that thought been a freak will heal you from your ex marriage. You did the same going than I do because you wanted to heal your abuse but you see Buddy, yours started when you were married and you only stayed 5 years in that sick relationship but you become a freak for another 5 years so now you are healed and you want to be exclusive. Buddy I can't, I refused to have kids because I didn't want to hurt my kids like my dad did me. I refused to marry so I don't have to use a woman like mom was used. Buddy, I am 50 years old, I have been destroyed and I destroyed myself for 45 years... Buddy why do you think I am healed or why do you want to destroy your life thinking you can heal me? If I follow your step Buddy, I need another 40 years to heal and may be I can be exclusive and truly to you My Buddy, My Life, My True Love.

CHAPTER

Eleven

Reason #11: Terminal Uniqueness

The W.A.S may feel like they are different.

They deserve something more special that others might not.

The usual rules just don't apply to them.

Therefore they are free to reward themselves outside their primary relationship whenever they want to.

Nikky and Tom met online chatting back to back then exchanged numbers then took it out of the online game.

Nikky is a very intelligent woman with an amazing personality.

Nikky is the lady that not only has a beautiful body shape, she got them Indian texture hair, very black, silky and straight.

Tom on the other is basic, we can give it a seven plus. He is average height with a starting alopecia where the light keeps reflecting out of the way.

He is extremely confident in everything about him.

Nikky was absolutely impressed by his self respect and self confidence. She thought we need more men like that.

They started to date and they got along pretty well.

Nikky traveled a lot for work but every time she is in town she is with Tom.

Tom on the other hand is a judge that works for the Immigration services and constantly showed respect by all the foreign refugees and asylees he met daily.

Those people feared him since his decision is a life sentence or a blessing for them.

With the new immigration reforms Tom has been more sollicitated then before so he hired an assistant.

Reynah was in her early twenties, very energetic and goal oriented.

Nikky met her during the recruiting video interview and she likes her. She told Tom to hire her because she has a "je ne sais quoi" about her that was so sparkling.

Tom didn't really care about the sparks but he liked the fact that she was inexperienced and he could be the boss once again and control her as he kind of starved for that behavior.

Reynah was punctual, Professional regardless of her young age, she was determined to be grown, don't ask me what that means.

Tom quickly became impressed with her capacity to learn and apply all his principles.

Within a few weeks it was frequent to hear Tom favorite say "check with Reynah".

Nikky never was concerned or felt insecure with Reynah's growing dependability of Tom.

A few times she actually took Raynah out for lunch and enjoyed a nice fresh conversation with her. It was easy to like Reynah.

Tom was not a Saint when it comes to women but Reynah was never a target for him, she was more like his daughter.

The country was engaging into this intense negotiations of refugees from Africa and Tom was about to get busy.

He invited Nikky for a romantic dinner before times became too hard to catch up with each other.

Tom out of nowhere proposed to Nikky in the restaurant! She sais YES!

They decided to stay engaged for about a year and will. proceed with the marriage.

Tom realized he could be a Governor, simple fact with social media, he was now reknowed on the country.

His follower was about a few millions.

He has his own show on national television.

Congress was scared of him.

He shared his excitement for his new finding journey to Nikky. To his surprise, Nikky dismissed the idea of him entering into politics.

She told him that it will stress their marriage and will expose them to haters.

Tom never knew Nikky was not ambitious. He thought she is getting cold feet or she is very selfish or insecure.

He tried again and she responded the same way.

Tom decided that he needs someone more submissive, a woman who respect her husband.

Nikky started to think she is all that but he needs a better half.

While brainstorming about his situation, he realized that his solution was right there the entire time..

Reynah!

Tom called Reynah in his office and ask her what was she thinking of his career change.

Reynah got exited automatically and start to play campaign manager.

That's all Tom needed to make a major decision in his life.

The opinion of Reynah.

Suddenly Nikky was no longer important to him. To his eyes she was nothing but a hater and he deserves better.

He kept Reynah working long hours till one day, he felt that it was so late, he will feel secure if he could drop her.

Tom took Reynah he that night and slept with her.

He was so bold, he spent the night and drove back to his office in the morning with him.

In that garage was Nikky, very stressed out. Looks like she never slept, worried about her Man.

She thought they must have been working so late and may have spent the night at work.

She realized Reynah's car was still in the parking lot but not Tom.

She thought probably they went grab some coffee.

Tom was still not answering nor returning her worried calls.

About fifteen minutes later, they pulled up on the parking lot.

The way they were closed, sitting in the car, left no doubt on what may have taken place.

She still asked Tom, what happened last night.

He answered: everything you never done! And he walked away holding confused Reynah hands.

Wow!

CHAPTER

Twelve

Reason #12: Unfettered Impulse

The W.A.S may never have even thought about cheating until an opportunity suddenly presented itself.

Then, without even thinking about what infidelity might do to their relationship, they went for it.

Not another explanation possible.

Those will be differentiated by guilt, personal confusion; difficulty to even explain why!

Like it just happened! That's all I know!

Another night in this cold and humid ER. I brought my charger today at least so I can catch up with shows on Netflix. We have been strangely slow since we required payment up front from uninsured patients. I do not agree with this decision but it's none of my business.

One day, I will move to Europe or America and start my life all over.

"Hey Claire, my beautiful Claire, how are you tonight?"

"I am doing great, Jean-Pierre. How about you?"

"I am good, beautiful he answered with his eyes all over my body. Ready for an amazing night?"

"Sure Jean-Pierre"

I hurried myself in the building, this guy has a way to creep me out.

The way he looks at me constantly raises the hair on the back of my head.

I know he likes me but I am not ready for him nor anyone else.

Since Baptiste I decided to go on celibacy and work on myself. No more cheaters again.

The night was going as usual till about 1am, we had a call that an ambulance was on the way from the US Embassy. Apparently one of their visitors felt sick.

Of course I am the only one that speaks English on this shift.

"Nurse Claire, we will need your services"

"Off course Dr Bah"

I knew my Netflix night was canceled.

Within 20 minutes of the call they were able to show up.

A white man looking kind of gray came out, he seemed really sick.

"Nurse Claire, please introduce yourself and all of us and let him know that we are going to take good care of him"

Which I did...and we did took care of him.

★ ★ ★

Today I am crying all I can, I have no more tears and my eyes are burning.

Ed stayed in the hospital for an entire week so I did it too. He was very sick and caught typhoid fever. The fever was so high he lost his memory and the use of his legs.

The US Embassy wanted to evacuate him but he refused stating that he wants to stay in our hospital to complete his care. Personally it was not a safe transfer if he would have agreed to it.

We got close and closer.

He made me smile again

Ed made my dreams come true, I wanted him to take me to the US but he wanted to stay with me in my country.

What we ended up doing.

We lived together for 5 years, I love him with all my heart. Ed was a true romantic, he taught me how to drive and bought my first car.

We just celebrated our 1st home together.

We were just talking 3 nights ago about a baby.

I know our baby will be so cute, curly hair, light brown eyes and may be milky chocolate skin complexion.

All this will never happen probably never any baby for me.

My cousin Georgina came from the village to the party we organized for the cremallaire.

She stayed an extra week and slept with Ed.

Yes you read it right, slept with Ed, like Ed cheated on me! After five years of a committed, loyal and trustworthy relationship.

How did we ended up here.

I need someone to kill me now, I don't have any reasons to live.

"Ed why my Love?" I asked him.

"Claire, I never cheated on you, trust me please.

I knew how hurt you got when your ex cheated on you. I knew how much you despised being cheated on. I knew how much you hate cheaters. I knew how you reacted to even a movie with a cheater. Claire I would have never done that on purpose. I am so sorry. I didn't mean to hurt you. I was drunk. Georgina came and laid next to me when you were cleaning up the kitchen. She said you sent her to check on me. She brought me a drink that she claimed you gave her for me. Claire I love you and if you give me a chance I promise you. I WILL NEVER NEVER EVER AGAIN HURT YOU.

As I look at Ed, my heart is on fire, never I thought Ed could have been a cheater.

Ed didn't had a chance to cheat on me but I saw Georgina on him naked on my bed about to ride my husband

"Claire, trust me I will never be that careless. I will never drink again, you are all I need my Love, I am sorry".

Not sure what Claire will decide but to me Ed is not a cheater. He is a good man and good man make mistake or any W.A.S is as weak as it comes.

Closing

No way can we explain the behaviors of a cheater nor the reaction of the cheated.

Most importantly we owe to ourselves to select our partners with the most wise reason possible.

A person capable of making "you" want to be the best "you" can be, a person making you speak from a place of softness, a person making you go above and beyond is a person worthy of your Love. Before we can Love others we have to love ourselves. Are we treated with respect? Are we appreciated? Are we settling because of lack of self esteem? Are we ready for a relationship? What are we bringing on the table? What are our expectation? So many questions that we need to answer before considering engaging into a relationship.

It's not always the fault of the cheater, several time the cheated on played a huge role in that ending.

We need to be real with ourselves and pay attention to obvious red flags.

It's good to be honest but not naive.

Good luck to all relationships and hope we show each other more respect toward our engagements and commitments.